LAMBSLIDE

by **Ann Patchett**

illustrated by Robin Preiss Glasser

HARPER
An Imprint of HarperCollinsPublishers

To Robin Preiss Glasser.
Thank you for inviting me to the party —A.P.

For Kate Jackson and Susan Katz, with gratitude
for all the years of loving support —R.P.G.

Library of Congress Cataloging-in-Publication Data
Names: Patchett, Ann, author. | Preiss Glasser, Robin, illustrator.
Title: Lambslide / by Ann Patchett; illustrated by Robin Preiss Glasser.
Description: First edition. | New York, NY: Harper, an imprint of
    HarperCollins Publishers, [2019] |
Summary: A flock of lambs mishears the word "landslide" as "lambslide" and begins
    a campaign to have one built for them on the farm.
Identifiers: LCCN 2018034254 | ISBN 9780062883384 (hardback)
Subjects: | CYAC: Sheep—Fiction. | Animals—Infancy—Fiction. | Domestic animals—
    Fiction. | Farm life—Fiction. | Humorous stories. | BISAC: JUVENILE FICTION /
    Animals / Farm Animals. | JUVENILE FICTION / Humorous Stories. |
    JUVENILE FICTION / Imagination & Play.
Classification: LCC PZ7.1.P3765 Lam 2019 | DDC [E]—dc23 LC record available
    at https://lccn.loc.gov/2018034254

The artist used ink and watercolor to create the illustrations for this book.
Typography by Jeanne L. Hogle
19 20 21 22 23 SCP 10 9 8 7 6 5 4 3 2 1
❖
First Edition

On the farm there was a flock of lambs who believed the sun came up in the morning because they were ready to get up and play and set at night because they were sleepy and ready for bed.

They thought the grass grew to please them . . .

and the rain fell to annoy them . . .

and the only reason butterflies fluttered by
was so lambs could chase them.

Everything was about the lambs,
as far as the lambs were concerned.

One day Nicolette Farmer announced to her Farmer family,
"I'm going to run for class president today!"
Mrs. Farmer said, "You'll win by a landslide!"
This meant her mother thought she'd win by a lot.

But the lambs thought she said, "You'll win by a lambslide!"
This was exciting news.

"Where is the lambslide?" the lambs asked their mother.

"There is no lambslide," their mother said. "Now will you please let me finish eating the lawn?"

The lambs were disappointed.
They wanted a lambslide.

"Every place we have to play is too flat," the first lamb said.
"No one can have fun in a flat meadow."

"The pigs get to play in the mud," the second lamb said. "We never get to play in the mud."

"That's because we aren't supposed to get our wool dirty," said the third lamb. The third lamb always did exactly as he was told.

"The horses get to go on fun rides with the Farmers.
We never get to go ANYWHERE."

The grumpy group of lambs went back to their mother.
She knew the answer to pretty much everything.
"How do we get a lambslide?" they asked.

"First," she said, "you should see what the other animals think."

This seemed like a good idea, so the lambs
went to the chicken coop.
"Do you think we should have a lambslide?"
the lambs asked a chicken.

"I don't know," said the chicken. "Who would pay for it?"
The lambs hadn't thought about this.

"The Farmers," they said, because the Farmers paid for everything. Lambs didn't have money.

"It's all right with me," said the chicken, "as long as it doesn't mean I get less chicken feed."

"Do you think we should have a lambslide?"
the lambs asked a goat.

"Would goats be allowed on the slide?" the goat inquired.
The lambs hadn't thought about this, but they didn't see why not.

"It's going to be a very big lambslide. There will be plenty of room for everyone."

"Then it sounds like loads of fun to me!" answered the goat.

"Do you think we should have a lambslide?" the lambs asked a pig.

"Will it cover up any of my muddy places?" asked the pig.
The lambs hadn't thought about where the lambslide would go.
They looked around the farm.

"It will be built right next to the barn," they said with authority.

"There's no mud there," said the pig, "so a lambslide is fine with me."

Now that the chicken and the goat and the pig had agreed that a lambslide would be a positive addition to the farm, the lambs asked their mother what they should do next.

"What do *you* think you should do next?" asked their mother, who thought lambs should figure things out for themselves whenever possible.

"Eat clover?" asked the first lamb.

"Run through the field?" asked the second lamb.

"Ask the Farmers?" asked the third lamb.

"I think letting the Farmers know how you feel is the best idea," said their mother.

The lambs decided to make some signs for the Farmers, but they weren't very good at it. So Nicolette helped them when she returned home.

She was, after all, now the president of her class.

The Farmers looked at the signs.
They were impressed that the lambs had
thought things through so carefully.

The Farmers decided that the whole farm should vote on whether or not there should be a lambslide.

When all the votes were counted,
the lambslide had won by a landslide.

Mr. and Mrs. Farmer thought about how to make the lambslide strong
enough for the cows and wide enough for the horses.

It needed to be long enough and fast enough to make it fun for the lambs. They put a big, soft haystack at the bottom so everyone would have a nice landing.

The lambs went down the lambslide
again and again and again.